How can we make beautiful cupcakes?

Written by Sally Morgan
Illustrated by Emily Hunter-Higgins

Collins

What's in this book?

Listen and say

cupcake

sheep

spot

panda

Download the audio at www.collins.co.uk/839679

star

spider

tiger

ladybird

Rosa and Dad are making cupcakes.

Rosa isn't happy.

How can we make our cupcakes beautiful?

Put some icing sugar in a bowl.
Add some water. Make the icing.

Put the icing on the cupcake.

Now you can write on the cupcake.
Use an icing pen.

Can you write your name?

icing pen

Write the letters on the cupcakes.

You can draw on your cupcake, too.

Let's draw two eyes.
Now draw the mouth.

Let's draw a panda.

You can make the ears and eyes from chocolates.

You want:

Make a tiger face.

Put some orange and black icing on a cupcake. Add some sweets.

You want:

Can you make a spider cupcake?
A spider has got eight long legs.

You want:

This is a sheep cupcake.
The head is chocolate.

You want:

Let's make a birthday cupcake!

Put some icing on the cupcake.
Add some stars and a candle.

Let's make a ladybird cupcake.
Put red icing on the cupcake.

Add a head and eyes.
Add some spots. Can you count
the spots?

Let's make a bee and flower cupcake.
Make a red flower.
Make a yellow and black bee.

Picture dictionary

Listen and repeat

bowl

candle

chocolate

cupcake

icing

icing sugar

sweets

1 Look and match

Let's make spider cupcakes!

Let's make sheep cupcakes!

Let's make bee and flower cupcakes!

Let's make birthday cupcakes!

2 Listen and say

Collins

Published by Collins
An imprint of HarperCollins*Publishers*
Westerhill Road
Bishopbriggs
Glasgow
G64 2QT

HarperCollins*Publishers*
1st Floor, Watermarque Building
Ringsend Road
Dublin 4
Ireland

William Collins' dream of knowledge for all began with the publication of his first book in 1819.

A self-educated mill worker, he not only enriched millions of lives, but also founded a flourishing publishing house. Today, staying true to this spirit, Collins books are packed with inspiration, innovation and practical expertise. They place you at the centre of a world of possibility and give you exactly what you need to explore it.

© HarperCollins*Publishers* Limited 2020

10 9 8 7 6 5 4 3 2

ISBN 978-0-00-839679-4

Collins® and COBUILD® are registered trademarks of HarperCollins*Publishers* Limited

www.collins.co.uk/elt

British Library Cataloguing in Publication Data

A catalogue record for this publication is available from the British Library.

Author: Sally Morgan
Illustrator: Emily Hunter-Higgins (Beehive)
Series editor: Rebecca Adlard
Commissioning editor: Fiona Undrill
Publishing manager: Lisa Todd
Product managers: Jennifer Hall and Caroline Green
In-house editor: Alma Puts Keren
Project manager: Emily Hooton
Editor: Emma Wilkinson
Proofreaders: Natalie Murray and Michael Lamb
Cover designer: Kevin Robbins
Typesetter: 2Hoots Publishing Services Ltd
Audio produced by id audio, London
Reading guide author: Emma Wilkinson
Production controller: Rachel Weaver
Printed and bound by: GPS Group, Sloveni

MIX
Paper from
responsible sources

FSC
www.fsc.org

FSC™ C007454

Download the audio for this book and a reading guide for parents and teachers at www.collins.co.uk/839679